Kippy the Kangaroo Rat

Story by Riana Fisher
Illustrated by Nafisa Arshad

KIPPY
BOOKS

© Copyright Kippy Books 2023 - All rights reserved.

The contents of this book may not be reproduced, duplicated, or transmitted without direct written permission from the author. Under no circumstances will any legal responsibility or blame be held against the publisher for any reparation, damages, or monetary loss due to the information herein, either directly or indirectly.

Once upon a time, there was a kangaroo rat named Kippy. He lived in the desert and spent most of his days searching for food and building tunnels.

However, Kippy had a bad habit. He was selfish and never considered the feelings of others.

One day, while Kippy was out looking for food, he came across a family of mice who were struggling to build their home.

Kippy saw that they were having a hard time and did not offer to help them. Instead, he took all the food they had gathered and went on his way.

As Kippy continued to wander, he suddenly heard a loud scream. It was one of his friends, a fellow kangaroo rat, who had gotten caught in a trap.

Kippy ran to help him, and together they managed to free him. Kippy's friend was grateful and thanked him for coming to his rescue.

It was then that Kippy realized how wrong he had been. He had always taken things for granted and never considered the feelings or needs of others. His friend's gratitude made him realize that he needed to change his ways.

From that moment, Kippy made it a point to treat others as he wanted to be treated.

He started helping his neighbors, even if it meant sacrificing some of his own resources.

He befriended the mice family and helped them build their home. He looked out for his fellow kangaroo rats and made sure they were safe.

In return, Kippy found that the other animals in the desert started treating him with kindness and respect.

He had earned their trust, and they looked up to him as a role model.

Kippy had learned a valuable lesson about treating others with kindness and respect.

He realized that by being more considerate towards others, he could make a positive difference in their lives, as well as his own.

THE END

Printed in the USA
CPSIA information can be obtained
at www.ICGtesting.com
LVHW071146141023
760475LV00004B/2